THE SCORPION SECRET

Other titles in this series:

Attack of the Jaguar

THE SCORPION SECRET

M. A. Harvey

Chrysalis Children's Books

First published in the U.K. in 2003 by
Chrysalis Children's Books
an imprint of Chrysalis Books Group Plc,
The Chrysalis Building,
Bramley Road,
London W10 6SP, U.K.

This edition is distributed in the U.S. by Publishers Group West.

Text © M.A. Harvey 2003
Illustrations by Garry Walton

The right of M.A. Harvey to be identified
as the author of this work has been asserted.

ISBN 1 844580 50 4

Printed in Great Britain by Creative Print & Design (Wales) Ltd
10 9 8 7 6 5 4 3 2 1

CONTENTS

Desert Survival Test

Now Send Later Save as Draft Add Attachments Signature ▾ Options ▾ Rewrap

From: Xtreme adventure inc.
To: Trainee Operatives
Cc:
Bcc:
Subject: Desert Survival Training Test
chments: none
Verdana ▾ Medium ▾ B I U T | ≣ ≣ ≣ | ≣ ≣ ≣ ≣ | A ▾ ◇ ▾ | —

XTREME ADVENTURE INC.
confirms you are authorized to read this top secret
transmission.

To: Trainee operative.
Re: North African desert survival training test.

XTREME ADVENTURE INC. is an organization dedicated to
protecting the planet and those who inhabit it. Our operatives
are an elite squad who have proved their bravery, survival skills,
and brainpower. They can survive in the most dangerous, hostile
places on Earth, and we call on them for rescue missions so
tough that all others would fail.

Do you have what it takes to join us? We shall see.

This training manual contains an adventure story. Imagine that
you are kidnapped and abandoned in the desert, far from help, or
trapped in an ancient Egyptian tomb with your enemies at the
entrance. All that and more happened to 13-year-old David
Turner and his 18-year-old stepbrother Zak. This is their story.
We'll call it…

THE SCORPION SECRET

WILL YOU MAKE THE GRADE?

In each chapter of this story there are quizzes for you to complete. They will test your brainpower and visual skills.

As you're reading, keep a record of your answers to the puzzles and quizzes.

Then check your credit score at the back of this book to see if you are capable of joining **XTREME ADVENTURE INC.**

Finally, turn to page 126 to try for a place in our ELITE SQUAD.

WARNING

Trainees who look at the answers first fail automatically, since this shows lack of discipline and inability to follow instructions. These are serious flaws for XTREME ADVENTURE operatives.

Good luck to all trainees.
Chief of Field Operations

Shop of Surprises

David Turner awoke and lay in his room looking up at a small lizard clinging motionlessly to the blank ceiling of his uncle's apartment. Lizards did that in Egypt, like spiders back home. They occasionally came in and settled themselves in corners. They were harmless, and this one hadn't moved for ages. "Boring, like the rest of this dump," David thought grumpily. "Egypt, land of the Pharaohs, secret treasure, and mysterious mummies....But I don't get to see any of it."

He listened for noise in the apartment, but all he could hear was the muffled sound of his stepbrother Zak snoring in the next room.

When his mom had told David he was going to

stay with his uncle in Egypt for summer break, he had been thrilled. His uncle was an archaeologist, and David had heard family stories about him being a real adventurer, solving crimes and discovering long-lost ancient sites. David hadn't seen him in years, but he'd always imagined him as a dashing treasure hunter, like Indiana Jones. He thought of his uncle embarking on daring adventures and taking his brave young nephew along for the ride.

No such luck.

Although his uncle had turned out to be pleasant and kind, and did have some exciting stories to tell, he was also retired, and there were no new adventures in sight for David. The apartment where they were staying was in a small Egyptian town far from anywhere important.

It also turned out that David was going to have to share his vacation with his currently snoring stepbrother. Since David had last seen *him* he appeared to have turned into the world's nerdiest human, whose idea of a day's entertainment seemed to be reading a book on ancient Egyptian history, instead of actually going outside to see it. OK, he spoke pretty good Arabic, which had been useful for buying candy at the airport, but except for that he was a disappointment.

He'd turned into an adult....Boring!

Things had gotten much worse when their uncle was called away on urgent business in the Egyptian capital, Cairo, and had left them on their own for a few days.

"You two are sensible enough," he'd said. "You won't encounter any problems if you stay put until I get back."

That was fine for a grownup to say, but boredom had driven David to some underhand planning. He didn't feel like being sensible now. They'd been killing time in the apartment for two days, Zak with his head permanently in a book and David playing on his Game Boy. Now its batteries had run out and so had his patience.

He got dressed and went into the kitchen.

"Great, no bread. Zak said he was going to get some yesterday. Supernerd!" David griped, loudly enough to deliberately wake Zak, who shuffled out of his room.

"Hi, David," he mumbled and looked around. "There's no bread," he sighed.

"So eat a book," David remarked under his breath. Zak ignored this suggestion.

"What activities are you planning for us today?" David continued, and this time there was a spark of mischief in his eyes.

"Well, I have some studying to do. Maybe you could watch TV...." Zak began.

"Oh, yes. That'd be a treat, for my *birthday*!" David emphasized the final word.

"It's your birthday? Nobody told me!" Zak exclaimed. "Maybe they did and you forgot," David replied accusingly.

"Oops!" Zak replied. "I'm sorry, David. I'll make it up to you."

David fixed his big brother with one of his best "nobody loves me" looks.

"You wait here. I'll go and get something great for breakfast, and some new batteries for your Game Boy, too." Zak promised. He got dressed, grabbed his money belt, and hurried out of the apartment, down a set of stairs, and out to the street below.

"So far, so good," David thought, satisfied that his plan to prize his stepbrother away from his books was going smoothly so far.

Outside, Zak's feet stirred up powdery dust as he walked between the flat-fronted white buildings of the town.

"I like it here. It's real, not like some faked-up tourist park," he muttered to himself, as if replying to David's repeated criticisms that it was a "boring dump." His younger stepbrother was beginning to get on his nerves. David had obviously imagined Egypt to be like some kind of adventure movie, and seemed to expect Zak to conjure up mummies and treasures, when in fact Zak was drowning in exam work and had come out here to study as much as he could.

"Thirteen-year-olds...they've got no idea how much work is involved in exams. Still, I should have remembered my own brother's birthday," he thought guiltily. "Now, where can I buy some Game Boy batteries?"

He turned into the bazaar, a maze of alleyways and stalls, and noticed a doorway with statues

piled up outside it.

"Aha, this could be the place to find the ideal present for David, preferably something with a hideous legend or a curse attached to it; something that he can scare all his buddies with," Zak grinned.

Inside, what looked like ancient Egyptian statues lay around, all reproduction stuff for the tourist trade. He glanced at them, but at first he didn't see anything good enough for the gift. He moved through the shop and stepped into a courtyard filled with goods.

He was stopped in his tracks by a low growl. A tough-looking dog had stood up from a shadowy corner and was eyeing Zak suspiciously.

"OK, Rami." A young teenage boy stood up from a table and reassured the dog. "He is my dog. He won't harm you," the boy explained. "He is helping me in the shop."

"Sure," Zak replied, but he kept a wary eye on the dog just the same as he wandered around looking for something to fire David's vivid imagination.

"This is great," he remarked, picking up a small

statue of a figure in an ancient headdress. A giant scorpion lay at her feet.

"It's Serqet, the scorpion goddess, isn't it? It's a very good-quality copy."

"You are a scholar!" the boy declared.

"Not really, but I'm studying ancient history," Zak replied, secretly rather pleased at the effect he'd had.

"I am learning, too. English." The boy directed Zak to the table where a book lay open, marked *English-Arabic Dictionary*. Next to it was a map of Egypt and a sheet of questions in English. It seemed that Zak had interrupted the boy doing his homework.

"I'll give you a hand with this homework, OK?" Zak suggested, and had soon helped him complete all the answers.

"You are very kind," the boy said. "And you have chosen a good statue. I think it must be brand new, straight from the stonemason's yard. I am guessing it is a copy of something from the Scorpion Tomb." Zak looked blank, so the boy filled in the details. "An ancient tomb has been found near the town. They say there are scorpion pictures on its walls."

"Is this tomb a very recent find?" Zak asked. "I haven't heard anything about it."

"Oh, yes. They have only just put some objects from the dig in our town museum," the boy replied.

"The statue's ideal for my brother's birthday. I'll take it," Zak decided.

"I think I made a friend back there," he smiled to himself as he walked back through the bazaar alleys with the statue of the goddess Serqet under his arm. "Now to please my annoying little stepbrother at last with a taste of ancient Egypt."

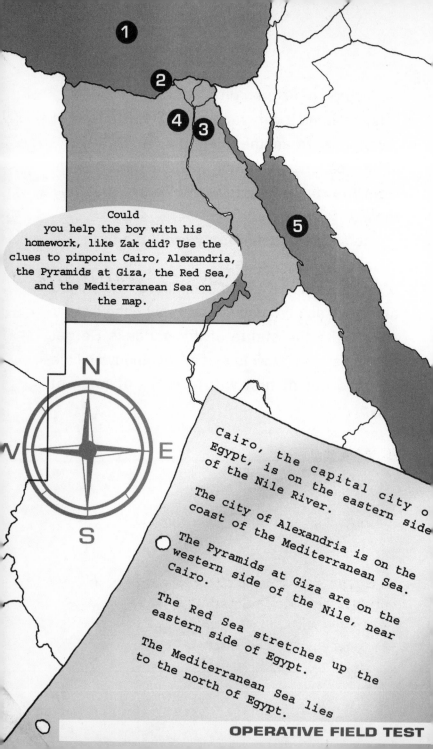

Could you help the boy with his homework, like Zak did? Use the clues to pinpoint Cairo, Alexandria, the Pyramids at Giza, the Red Sea, and the Mediterranean Sea on the map.

Cairo, the capital city of Egypt, is on the eastern side of the Nile River.

The city of Alexandria is on the coast of the Mediterranean Sea.

The Pyramids at Giza are on the western side of the Nile, near Cairo.

The Red Sea stretches up the eastern side of Egypt.

The Mediterranean Sea lies to the north of Egypt.

OPERATIVE FIELD TEST

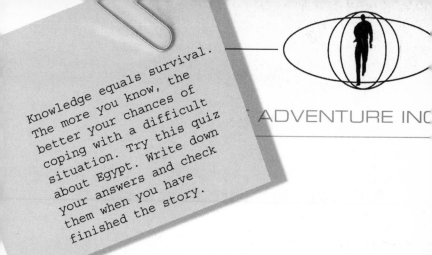

Knowledge equals survival. The more you know, the better your chances of coping with a difficult situation. Try this quiz about Egypt. Write down your answers and check them when you have finished the story.

XTREME ADVENTURE QUIZ 1

1. What is the Nile?
a) A river
b) A mountain
c) A city

2. Where is Egypt?
a) Southern Europe
b) North Africa
c) South Africa

3. Egypt lies next to the Mediterranean. What is the Mediterranean?
a) A mountain
b) A lake
c) A sea

4. What is the capital city of Egypt?

a) Copenhagen

b) Capetown

c) Cairo

5. Egypt has a large area of desert. What is a desert?

a) A swampy area

b) A very dry area

c) A thickly forested area

6.0000000000 The giant Suez Canal stretches across part of Egypt. What is the Suez Canal?

a) A man-made road

b) A man-made river channel

c) A man-made tunnel

Followed

"Oh, er, thanks, Zak," David said politely, when Zak handed him his present.

"She's a scorpion goddess. She will bring down the curse of the scorpion on anyone who deserves it," Zak explained. "But she protects those she favors."

"Cool!" David gasped delightedly, and Zak knew that his statue present had worked.

"It's very realistic, isn't it?" Zak pointed out enthusiastically. "It's a copy of a statue found in a local excavation, apparently. I'm surprised Uncle didn't mention the dig to us."

"Er, Zak. About my birthday..." David began.

"Say no more. I feel awful about forgetting it. I'm going to put away my books for the day and take you out to a cafe for breakfast. Come on, birthday boy," Zak grinned.

At the local café Zak told David all about the tomb dig he'd heard about that morning.

"Wow! A real ancient tomb!" David exclaimed excitedly. "Wouldn't it be great if we could see it? It would be something really exciting to tell everyone when we get back home!"

"Your wish is my command, oh birthday boy," Zak joked, and raised his cup of coffee to make a toast. "Here's to an exciting day! Let's find this town museum, make an impression, and see if we can visit the excavation site."

"Fantastic!" David agreed.

Eventually the waiter brought the check. "It's on me," Zak smiled, studying it.

"What's that written on the back?" David asked, peering at the check in Zak's hands.

Zak flipped it over and furrowed his forehead. "It says: 'Do not go home,'" he read. "That's weird. I don't think it can be a message for us." He called the waiter over and spoke to him in Arabic.

"He says he has no idea who wrote it or what it means. His check pad has been lying on the counter, so anyone could have done it. It's probably just a misunderstanding," he remarked. "Come on, let's get back."

They stepped from the shade into the street outside. A truck rattled by. A cat shot from one doorway to another, then up some outside stairs onto a flat roof above. It seemed to be a normal day in a small Egyptian town...until a man came out from a side alley. He walked behind them and, oddly, he seemed to be keeping pace with them.

"Zak, do you think he's following us?" David whispered, half-jokingly.

"We can soon find out," Zak smiled, thinking this was just a game between the two of them. He veered into an adjoining alley. "Hide in that doorway, like they do in spy movies," he pointed. He and David flattened themselves against a door in a pool of shade. To their amazement, the man walked past their hiding place a minute later, looking sharply ahead.

"Let's go back the way we came," David whispered, and they retraced their steps to the main street, only to find the man had himself doubled back by another route and was now

coming toward them, with what seemed to be an unfriendly expression. David glanced behind, where another man suddenly appeared from a side door, staring at them.

"What's going on?" Zak muttered as David plucked at his sleeve.

"Follow me," David urged and dodged across the road, pulling Zak along with him.

They made for the set of outside stairs they had seen the cat use minutes earlier. When they reached the top, flat roofs stretched before them, filled with clotheslines and flowerpots. The roofs were separated by low walls or trellises. Some had stairwells leading down into houses and courtyards below. Others had outside stairs leading to street level.

Their pursuers would soon catch up. They had to decide what to do, and fast. David quickly took in the scene.

"Follow me," he ordered once again.

"Yes, sir," Zak replied.

They leapt over low walls, avoiding trellises, crumbling stairwells, and in one case a sleeping dog, not daring to look back until they had found a flight of stairs that took them safely back down to another street.

This time it was deserted. They hid in shade for a moment, but no one appeared. Eventually they glanced at each other, then started to grin. "I think I had too much coffee at your birthday breakfast, little bro. It's made me kind of jumpy. There's no one following us," Zak laughed.

"Yeah, you're right, and I guess I've seen too many spy movies," David giggled. "But it was an adventure, wasn't it? We made a great team for a little while, didn't we? Turner and Turner, special agents!"

"Come on, superspy. Let's go back to the apartment," Zak replied. It was true, though, he thought to himself. For a moment back there, it had felt like they were a team, big brother and little brother, and it had been fun.

"Hey, Zak, you left the door open," David remarked when they reached the top of their stairwell. "Special agents don't do that."

"I didn't," Zak replied indignantly.

"Did," David replied. He pushed at the door, and it swung open to reveal a shocking mess. The contents of their uncle's apartment lay scattered across the floor.

"We've been robbed," Zak cried, bewildered. He moved through the apartment, shaking his head. "That's weird. I can't see anything missing," he muttered, then turned and wandered into David's room. "David, the statue I gave you..." he called out, then stopped.

"Don't tell me someone stole my present!" David gasped. "Why would...?"

His question was cut off as his arms were grabbed from behind by an unseen enemy. As he struggled, a gag was slipped over his mouth. He caught a glimpse of his brother being marched from the bedroom before the scene was blanked by some kind of sack being slipped over his head.

He felt his legs being kicked away from under him, and he fell.

Which route should David and Zak take across the rooftops, to reach safety in the street below?

OPERATIVE FIELD TEST 2

XTREME ADVENTURE QUIZ 2

1. Would you:

a) Stay in a crowded street?

b) Hide in a quiet alley?

2. Would it be best to:

a) Keep walking in a straight line toward your destination?

b) Make changes of direction?

3. Which would be the best option:

a) Try to get a secret glimpse of your pursuer in a shop window?

b) Turn around so your pursuer knows you have seen him?

4. To lose your pursuer, would you:
a) Go into a public toilet?
b) Go into a restaurant?

5. Would you:
a) Get on a bus?
b) Get into a taxi?

6. If you were in a car being followed, would you:
a) Drive home?
b) Drive to a shopping center?

Sound of Silence

David guessed they'd been bundled into a truck. He knew that type of engine noise: throaty, with a diesel tick. It must have been driven up to the door of their apartment building. That way nobody from the street would have seen them being bundled inside, their hands and feet tied up, their gagged heads hidden by burlap.

"Grmmmmh." Zak tried to make a sound through his gag, risking a beating if any captors were in the back of the truck with him. He didn't care about that. He was desperate to know if David was safe. "Gmmrr," came a muffled noise in reply. His little brother was somewhere close, gagged like him. Zak waited, but no one hit him or said anything. He guessed they were

31

on their own in the back.

The truck stopped three times (at traffic lights, David guessed), and occasionally the engine dulled enough for snatches of noise to float in from the Egyptian streets outside. Someone was shouting at passers-by from a bazaar market stall, selling leather bags. They heard gushing water, then some kids laughing and jabbering as they were let out of their classroom at recess. Then they heard the distinctive sound of the Muslim call to prayer coming from a mosque.

"I must stay focused," Zak urged himself. "I hope David doesn't do anything stupid."

"Wait and stay alert," David was thinking. "I hope Zak doesn't do anything crazy."

The brakes squealed and fresh air rushed in as the back of the truck was opened. Hands grabbed them and pulled them out. Briefly they heard a chisel ringing out as it hit what must have been a block of stone. There were snatches of Arabic:

"Get them inside, quickly."

"Go and tell the boss we got the statue but had to get the brothers, too."

They were taken indoors. It felt cooler and smelled musty. A door was opened, then shut. Somewhere in the background they could hear people arguing. Zak strained to listen but couldn't make out the words; the argument was going on too fast and too far away. When it ended he could pick out the occasional traffic horn sounding in the distance. "At least that probably means we're still in the town," he thought.

Suddenly a whisper sounded close by, not from inside the room but possibly through an open window.

"You must forget the statue. Do not seek it out." The English words hissed and then died away, as more footsteps sounded.

"Grrmmmh," Zak replied, trying to provoke more words, but none came.

David's head was spinning. They'd stolen his statue! But why? What was so special about it? He tried to picture it: a copy of a goddess in a headdress with a wicked-looking scorpion at her feet ready to sting her enemies. There was one slight chip, a small piece of damage that didn't matter. It made the copy look more authentic.

Footsteps and voices cut into his train of thought. The door opened. Hands grabbed them and they were carried back to the truck.

It was a bumpier ride this time, with less outside noise. They both guessed that meant they were going out into the dusty, rocky desert landscape that surrounded the town. Eventually the truck stopped. They were taken across to some other vehicle and pushed inside. Then a new sound started, and to their horror they both realized they were inside a helicopter.

David edged over, trying to find Zak. He wanted to be beside him if something awful was going to happen. Eventually they managed to position themselves back to back, and it was a relief to both of them to feel they weren't alone.

They flew for at least twenty minutes. Zak tried to count, partly as a way of controlling himself, but he kept losing concentration so he couldn't be sure of the timespan.

After a while the helicopter began to descend and they felt it land. Then the doors were opened and they felt a wave of chilly air. Evening was coming and the temperature was

plummeting outside.

They were lifted out and two of their captors spoke to each other:

"I will untie them."

"Are you sure? The boss said..."

"He only wants to scare them."

Someone untied Zak's hands and hissed in his ear, "Stay still until we are gone, or we will turn the copter around and land on you."

A similar warning was given to David. "Stay put until you can no longer hear us," he was told.

They both obeyed and stood motionless as the helicopter started up. They were terrified of the whirling blades they could not see. They could feel sand whipping into their legs and arms as it was kicked up by the machine.

Then the noise faded and was gone.

They blundered toward each other and between them they managed to untie their sacks and gags.

"Are you OK?" David gasped.

"Yes. You?" Zak asked anxiously.

"Just stiff," David grimaced. "Zak, about my birthday..."

"I know, I know. I wanted to give you a surprise, but, believe me, not one like this. The whole thing has something to do with your present, but I can't figure out what. I'm sorry," Zak apologized.

"Don't be. It's not your fault," David sighed.

He looked around, and his sigh became a groan. They were in the middle of a desolate landscape, strewn with rocks and sand but with no signs of life, not even plants. There was certainly no town in sight, or any evidence of humans. There was nothing on the horizon but emptiness, lit by a huge ball of sun that was sinking out of sight.

Night was coming, and the Turner boys were on their own in the middle of the desert.

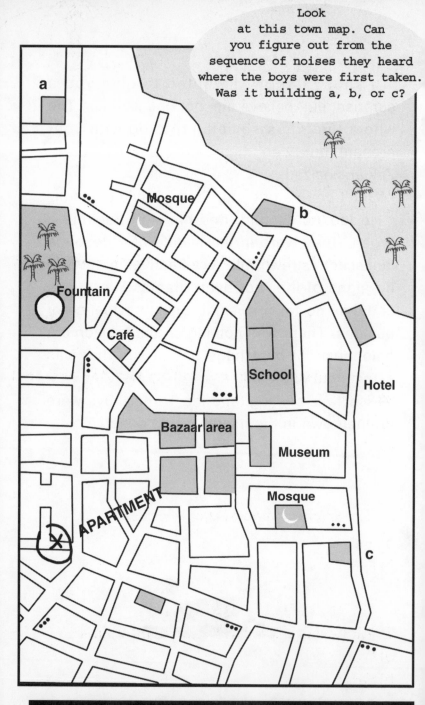

OPERATIVE FIELD TEST 3

The deserts of North Africa are dangerous, tough places. The more you know, the more chance you would have of surviving in David and Zak's situation. Try this desert quiz. Note your answers and check them when you have finished the story.

ADVENTURE INC

XTREME ADVENTURE QUIZ 3

1. In the desert it is hot during the day and cold at night.
a) True
b) False

2. The coolest time of day is at noon.
a) True
b) False

3. All deserts are filled with sand dunes.
a) True
b) False

4. Which would you be most likely to find in a North African desert?
a) A poisonous frog
b) A poisonous snake

5. Which would you find?
a) Sandflies
b) Treeflies

6. When wind whips sand and dust across the desert it is called:
a) A sandwind
b) A sandstorm

Into the Wilderness

"They've abandoned us in the middle of nowhere," David whispered, his voice quiet with shock.

"Looks that way," Zak muttered. "OK, we need to be practical," he said more loudly, trying hard to make his voice sound confident and in control, for his little brother's sake. He was struggling to think back now to all those adventure movies he'd seen when he was David's age. The heroes always used gadgets to get out of trouble.

"Equipment is what we need. David, what do you have in your pockets? Did you bring anything that might help us?" he asked.

"Um...a pencil, a penknife, a restaurant napkin, and a plastic bag of coins. How about you?" David asked.

"Well, let's see. I've got a small pocket mirror and a roll of film," Zak announced, laying them out on the ground along with David's few bits and pieces.

"And we've got the sacks and rope they used to tie us," David added brightly.

"Good. We have some equipment." Zak tried hard to sound jaunty, but he knew he wasn't kidding David. His little brother had seen those movies, too, and they both knew they needed water bottles, tents, boots....

"I'm going to have to admit that I have no idea what to do next," Zak thought to himself.

"I don't think he has any idea of what to do," David thought privately.

There was a glum silence between them before David came up with a suggestion. "I think we should begin to walk toward town. It will be better to walk out of the sun's glare, and the exercise will help keep us warm," he said.

"OK...I think that sounds like a good plan. Let's hope it's a moonlit night," Zak agreed. "But I'll tell you what. Before we start, give me the pencil. Let's make a list of what we both heard on our journey. It could be important, and if we don't do it now we'll forget the details."

"Yeah...yeah, that's a good idea," David replied.

By the time they had filled the napkin with notes, the temperature had plummeted and all daylight had gone. Above them, stars peppered the sky.

"See that bright star up there?" David pointed. "I think it's the North Star. I remember learning about it at school. The direction directly below it is north."

"I'm assuming we were flown south. It's just a guess, but there's a bigger stretch of desert to the south of the town. I think we should take a risk and go north," Zak suggested. David nodded. They both felt a little less helpless now they had thought of something practical.

It was hard walking through such a tough

landscape in virtual darkness. There were rocks to trip over, soft sand, and lots of potholes. Occasionally they heard a fennec fox screech, and once there was an unidentified rustle close by. Zak knew there were likely to be poisonous snakes out here in the wilderness, but he didn't mention it to David. David knew, too, but didn't say anything to Zak. They trudged on, with no sign of any lights in the distance.

At last David stopped. "Zak, I think we need to plan for tomorrow. When the sun comes up it's going to be too hot to walk. We should make a shelter that will give us some shade, and think about how to get some water."

Put like that, these problems seemed virtually insurmountable to Zak. He could translate hieroglyphics and date just about any ancient Egyptian object, but making a shelter? Getting water? He had no idea, and there was going to be no way to hide it.

"I can remember a few survival tips from TV shows," David said hesitantly. "Maybe now it's time to see if they work." He sounded nervous. He knew Zak wasn't an outdoor type, but he didn't want to show him up. He didn't have to worry. Zak was relieved that David wasn't expecting him to be Indiana Jones.

"I knew it was a good idea to come to Egypt with you!" Zak grinned, and David laughed, for the first time in hours.

They walked on until they found an outcrop of rocks. David tied together the ropes they had carried with them and fixed them between the rocks like a clothesline. "This'll be our shelter when the sun comes up," he explained. "We'll drape the two sacks over the rope and weigh the edges down with stones. Then we'll crouch under them out of the glare."

"Brilliant!" Zak congratulated him.

"Yeah, not bad," David smiled. "Water is going to be trickier, though. We're too late to get it tonight. Tomorrow we're going to have to dig a hole and put some kind of container in the bottom of it. Then we'll use my plastic bag to cover over the hole and hope that condensation gathers under the plastic and drips into the container...."

Zak's heart sank. This crackpot idea for water-

collecting sounded about as impossible as them finding a diner for breakfast in the morning. He remembered actors in old desert movies, staggering, and croaking around: "Water, water!" and mistaking mirages for sparkling lakes. What would those hard Special Forces survival types do in this situation? Probably drink their own pee or something, he thought to himself. It was clear that lack of water was quickly going to be their worst problem out here in the desert wasteland.

The night came to an end with a spectacular sunrise. It was beautiful, but they knew it signaled the onset of blistering temperatures.

"We need to get under cover. It's about to heat up," Zak advised. They hunched under the burlap as best they could.

"Hey, I've remembered something!" Zak cried triumphantly. He took out the film roll from his pocket. "Give me your penknife," he asked. He turned away and fiddled around, then turned back to David, who burst out laughing. Zak was wearing some of the film around his head, with two slits cut for his eyes.

"Ta-da! Sunglasses!" he announced. "I'm going to make you a pair, too."

"They're fantastic," David agreed, still giggling. "Did you read that idea in a survival book or something?"

"On the back of a cereal box, little brother, and I have to warn you: it's my only survival skill other than making you laugh by looking ridiculous. Anyway, I think I'm going to get up and stretch," he announced. He crawled out of the shelter and sat on a rock, took his shoes and socks off, and wriggled his toes to get his circulation going. Without thinking, he put his bare foot down on the ground, and suddenly felt a sharp penetrating pain.

"Aargh!"

David rushed out into the open. His brother was clutching his foot and grimacing. "I've been stung, or bitten, or something!" Zak yelped.

"Maybe there's a creature down there, under the rock," David cried. "Move out of the way, Zak. I can't see...."

"Is it a snake?" Zak panicked.

"I don't know. Whatever it was, it's gone," David whispered, feeling terrified. He'd wanted some adventure, but not like this. They crawled back under the burlap.

"David, listen. You've got to be strong for me, now," Zak muttered. He didn't add what he was thinking, that if he had been bitten by a snake, he would be dying some time soon. His toe felt as if it was burning.

"Take a close look at my foot, will you? Can you see puncture marks?" he asked.

"No...no, there's nothing," David confirmed. Zak lay back, and blew out his breath.

"Do you feel dizzy?" David asked.

"No, not yet," Zak sighed. "I'll be OK. We'll just have to wait...."

"It's my fault," David blurted out.

"Of course it's not," Zak insisted.

"You don't understand. I told you it was my birthday, and it wasn't. I wanted you to stop working, that's all. Then you brought me that scorpion goddess. She's sent me a punishment," David babbled.

"Calm down, calm down," Zak insisted. "Look,

I'm glad it's not your birthday. It'd be a rotten one, wouldn't it? And that curse stuff is just old nonsense, honest."

He was feeling dizzy now, but he didn't want David to know. "Go outside and take another good look for a creature. But be careful!" he warned.

"OK, if you're sure. Wait here!' David agreed, and crawled out of the shelter for another search.

"I'm not planning to go anywhere for a while," Zak murmured, and lay back on the ground. A few minutes later he heard David's excited voice:

"Zak, Zak. I can see something!"

"Does it have fangs, or a sting in its tail?" Zak asked fearfully.

"No, no. I can see something moving on the horizon," David explained.

"Oh, that's probably a mirage," Zak sighed. "Is it shimmering like a lake of cool water? It's not real, David. It's a trick of the desert light...."

"It's not that....Wait a minute. I'll use the pocket mirror," David muttered. "I'll try to signal by getting the sun to flash off the mirror." He angled it up and down, to try to reflect a sun ray. There was definitely a small cloud of dust eddying in the distance. It was approaching.

"There are people on camels!" David cried out. "Zak, we're going to be rescued!...Zak?"

Zak didn't reply.

> Which desert animal bit or stung Zak?

Egyptian cobra bite:
Pain and swelling, blistering, puncture wound visible, soon the victim has difficulty breathing. Bite can be fatal.

Wasp sting: Immediate stabbing pain, redness.

Scorpion sting:
No wound visible, burning sensation, possibly developing into a prickling skin sensation, dizziness, cramps, inability to talk or walk properly.

Mosquito bite: No immed symptoms. Itching and blistering later.

Carpet viper bit
Constant bleedin at the site of the bite, which is caused by the poison affecting the blood vessel pain, puncture wounds visible. Bite can be fata

If you were lost in the North African desert you would need to know some survival skills. Try this quiz to see how you would shape up. Choose option a or b. Keep a note of your answers so you can add up your score when you finish reading the story.

XTREME ADVENTURE QUIZ 4

1. Which would be the most important thing to do in the desert?

a) Wrap something around your head

b) Wrap something around your hands

2. Where would you be most likely to find water?

a) In a patch of desert where there are lots of red rocks

b) In a patch of desert where there are lots of plants growing

3. If your traveling companion was bitten by a snake, would you:

a) Suck out the poison for them

b) Tell them to lie still while you get help

4. It is very dangerous for a human body to go without enough water. What is this called?

a) Dehydration

b) Defibrillation

5. Where do scorpions like to hide?

a) In shady places

b) In patches of hot sunshine

6. In the hot desert it is better to:

a) Wear short sleeves and shorts

b) Wear long sleeves and long pants

A Helping Hand

Gama, the leader of a small Bedouin family group, saw a strange sight as he and his two sons trotted their camels over toward the flashing signals they could make out on the horizon. There was a boy waving madly, with some kind of film wrapped around his head, and there was a young man lying under some sacks. Still, he would help them if it was possible, even if they did look like a pair of crazies. The young man could speak some Arabic, though not very intelligibly. He said he'd been stung or bitten on the foot but couldn't say by what. He was almost passing out.

They lifted the crazies onto their camels and

took them back to camp, a few goatskin tents in a circle, with some tethered camels and goats nearby. Gama had settled his family temporarily here so that he could go into town to trade for some supplies and tools. Following Bedouin custom, the women of the group pulled their veils over their faces and ran into one of the tents when they saw that Gama had brought home strangers.

David was ushered into a tent with Zak, and Gama examined the throbbing foot.

"I've got a raging headache, and prickling over my skin, and I'm sweating like a pig," Zak muttered. He tried to get up, but Gama gently pushed him down.

"I think a scorpion has stung you. It is making you restless, affecting your thoughts as well as your body," Gama explained. He called to a child who was peeking curiously through the tent flap. The little boy rushed off and returned with an earthenware pot full of a yellowy paste that Gama smeared on Zak's foot.

"I'll be all right," Zak smiled weakly at David. "Gama says things could be rough for the next with Zak, but Gama said that his brother would be tended to through the night, and David must get some sleep. It was true that tiredness had crept up on him until his limbs ached, but when he fell asleep he dreamed restlessly of scorpions.

The next morning he rushed across to see Zak. "Hi," his brother grinned. He was sitting up and feeling much better. David felt a huge rush of relief.

"I have some interesting information, Agent Turner," Zak said, imitating James Bond. "Gama says he has heard of the Scorpion Tomb. Apparently he and his sons once rode past the excavation and saw men with guns."

"Guns? Why would excavators want guns?" David pondered.

Zak shrugged. "Gama says he'll take us to town tomorrow. I don't think we'll be in danger as long as we forget the statue."

The brothers glanced at each other, then said no more.

The next morning they set off with Gama toward the town. He lent them long cloths twenty-four hours or so, and then it'll pass. He says it was probably a scorpion. The paste is made from crushed plants, and is the best cure he knows."

"I'm sorry," David whispered. "I really am. I was being so selfish when I pretended it was my birthday."

"Don't be sorry. What with your burlap tent and your mirror trick, you probably saved my life back there," Zak said, squeezing his arm. "Gama says we're not all that far from town. It's a day's camel ride north. We were right to go north, you see. We would have made it home in the end!" Zak attempted a smile. His little brother had been impressive out in the desert; by contrast he felt that he'd been useless.

Gama brewed sweet mint tea, the traditional welcoming drink of the Bedouins. Rounds of warm flat bread were brought in, newly baked on the fire outside.

Afterward David slept in one of the other tents, curled up on cushions and covered in a warm goat-hair blanket. He had wanted to stay to tie around their heads and faces, protection from sun and sand dust. After a while he pointed to the horizon, where a slope and rock face were in distant view.

"That is the Scorpion Tomb," he explained. "The town lies just to the west." Roofs soon came into view, and when they reached the town they parted. "Good luck to you," Gama said. "Here our ways part. If you would like to visit my family again, we will be camped a day's ride south of the town for another week or so. You will be welcome."

The apartment was just as they had left it, a mess with the door still unlocked. No one had been in since they'd been kidnapped.

"They got what they wanted," Zak murmured.

"The statue," David added. "And to scare us." He looked at Zak. "I don't think we should give up so easily," he said fiercely, voicing at last what he had been thinking since they had spoken in Gama's tent.

"I thought you would say that," Zak smiled. "You want to find your statue."

"Don't you?" David asked.

Zak nodded. "Yes I do. I don't like being bullied, and I don't like my little brother's birthday being ruined by thugs," he said.

"Well, it wasn't my birthday...." David muttered, embarrassed.

"They didn't know that," Zak grinned. "Time for the napkin, I think!"

David pulled out the napkin with the list of noises written on it, the ones they'd remembered hearing when they were first kidnapped and driven through town. Zak spread out a map of the town streets.

"All we need to do is compare the sequence of noises we wrote down to the town map. Now, let's see...." They both came to the same conclusion at the same time.

"We were taken to that building." Zak pointed to a shape on the map.

"Let's go back there now, under cover of darkness," David urged.

"You are unstoppable, Agent Turner," Zak grinned, and reached for a flashlight.

They slid back into the darkened streets and, taking all the back routes they could, they reached the building unseen. It turned out to be a stonemason's yard and workshop. David threw a pebble over its wall to disturb any guard dogs on the other side. There was no response, so they climbed over.

There were stones piled in the yard, ready for chiseling, together with finished and unfinished statues copied from various periods in ancient Egyptian history. Zak shone the flashlight around until he saw what he was looking for. He shone the light on a row of finished statues, all of the same scorpion goddess, even more perfect-looking than David's present. Some statues at the end of the row had been smashed and a hammer lay nearby, indicating that the job wasn't finished yet.

"They made lots of statues. Then they changed their mind. I wonder why?" David remarked. Zak went along the remaining row of statues, studying them closely. "Yours is very slightly different from all these others. There it is." He picked one out. "Yours isn't perfect because it isn't a copy, David. It's the real thing. I'm sure of it now," he muttered.

"But why would it be hidden here?" David asked, puzzled.

Zak stood up, looking grim. "My bet is it's stolen property. That's why someone wanted it back badly enough to come looking for it. I think this could be serious, and I think it's time we got some help. I suggest we go to the local museum tomorrow and see if we can find someone to talk to."

David nodded. He knew his big brother was right. They'd had an adventure and managed to survive on their own, but now it was time to get back-up.

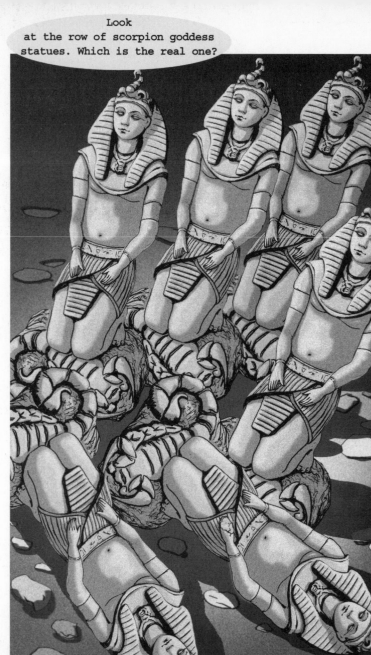

Bedouin people of the North African deserts have their own unique way of life. The more you understand, the better you will get along with them. Test your knowledge in this quiz, keeping a record of your answers.

XTREME ADVENTURE QUIZ 5

1. Bedouins live in tents in the desert.
a) True
b) False

2. Bedouins move around from place to place, looking for good grazing for their animals.
a) True
b) False

3. Bedouins mainly use horses to carry them from place to place.
a) True
b) False

4. Bedouins usually wear shorts and t-shirts.
a) True
b) False

5. Bedouins speak Gaelic.
a) True
b) False

6. Bedouins welcome visitors with cups of tea.
a) True
b) False

Cornered

David and Zak were waiting outside the museum early next morning. Neither had slept well, though they had hidden the statue inside one of Zak's socks and it seemed unlikely that anyone would notice immediately that it was missing from the stoneyard. Even so, they both felt relieved when the museum doors opened promptly and they hurried inside. In a back room they found a small exhibition of recent finds from near the town. There were only a few minor ones from the Scorpion Tomb.

"They haven't put any really good pieces on display, have they? And they've put it all at the back of the museum in this dusty old corner, as if they don't want anyone to notice," David whispered to Zak.

"Maybe if they're still working on it they want to avoid being overrun by tourists," Zak suggested. "But here's something really strange. Someone has written in these museum notes that the tomb was robbed in ancient times and little of worth remains. It says specifically that there were no movable statues found. That's weird...."

"We should find someone to talk to about it," David proposed. He gestured to a door at the back of the exhibition, marked EXCAVATION DIRECTOR. DOCTOR SIMMONS. He tried the handle.

"David, don't just barge in!" Zak began, but the door had already swung open. Inside, a tall blond-haired man sat with his back to them, studying the screen on a laptop computer. He spun around as they entered.

"What on earth do you think you're doing? This is my private office!" He stood up, looking outraged.

"Please excuse the interruption. We're looking for someone to speak to about the Scorpion Tomb. Have you worked on the dig?" Zak asked, putting on his most charmingly polite voice. The man stared at him.

"The exhibition is outside. Leave my office," he snapped frostily. At that moment David saw something. He half-turned to warn Zak, but it was too late. His big brother had taken out the statue of the scorpion goddess.

"We believe this could be from the site," Zak announced. "We bought it from a shop in good faith, and then we were..."

He stopped speaking when he saw the look on the man's face. Doctor Simmons glared angrily at the statue and then at Zak. "You are thieves!" he shouted loudly. "This was stolen by you!"

"No, not at all. Let me explain...." Zak floundered on, but David was yanking his arm. "Thieves!" the man was screaming. He was lunging toward them.

"Run!" Zak shouted.

They ran, past an open-mouthed museum receptionist and out the door into the street. "Thieves!" they heard the man shout behind them.

"Go into the bazaar!" David cried. They dived

through an archway into the narrow maze of stalls and ran on. They could still hear the voice in the distance.

"Stop the thieves!"

Then they heard the bark of a dog and, glancing back, they caught sight of a fierce-looking creature bounding after them. "They've set dogs on us!" David squealed. On they ran, around a blind corner....

"Just our luck. It's a dead end," Zak panted as they were forced to stop against a high wall. They turned to face the dog's fangs.

"Rami," a girl's voice rang out, and the dog stalled and turned. A girl, no more than seven or eight, had entered the narrow alley. "Rami, good dog," she said in Arabic, and then she turned her brown eyes on David and Zak. "Are you OK?" she asked. "Rami wouldn't hurt anyone. Is one of you Zak?"

"Yes..." Zak replied in Arabic. "Rami; I've heard that name before...."

"In the shop, probably," the girl explained. "My name is Layla. My big brother Hassan sold you a statue."

"Your brother!" Zak gasped.

The little girl looked behind her shoulder. Voices in the bazaar were taking up the cry of "Thieves!"

"We must find safety. Please, follow me," she urged, and led them swiftly through a doorway into a deserted courtyard, then up some steps onto the rooftops, where she found a hidden corner. They crouched out of view and talked. Zak translated for David.

"My brother told me what happened when he sold you the statue. He doesn't usually work in the shop. He was just minding it that morning for a neighbor, Mr. Rashi, who owns it," the girl explained. "He was so pleased to sell something, but when Mr. Rashi came back and found the statue gone, he was very angry and told Hassan he was going to get it back from you."

"Why was Mr. Rashi so angry?" Zak asked.

"I don't know. He said he couldn't tell me everything because it would be too dangerous," Layla replied, crestfallen. "I know that Mr. Rashi made Hassan work in his stonemason's yard to pay him back for losing the statue. Then last night my brother crept out and didn't come back. He thinks nobody noticed, but I saw him go. I think he's in trouble. When I saw you running I thought...well, maybe you could help me find him. Hassan said you were very smart, Zak."

There were tears in her eyes.

"Zak, can you ask Layla something? Does Hassan know any people at the museum?" David asked. Zak passed on the question, and the little girl nodded. "He said he met the tomb digger, at the shop," she confirmed.

"I have a feeling Dr. Simmons is mixed up in the statue theft. I saw something suspicious in his office," David muttered.

Zak knelt down and looked into the little girl's worried eyes. It was clear that she was terrified for her brother.

"We will find Hassan, I promise," he said. "Whatever it takes, we will find him."

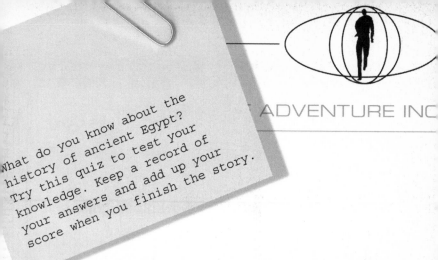

What do you know about the history of ancient Egypt? Try this quiz to test your knowledge. Keep a record of your answers and add up your score when you finish the story.

ADVENTURE INC

XTREME ADVENTURE QUIZ 6

1. In ancient Egypt a ruler was called:
a) Fairo
b) Pharaoh

2. Ancient Egyptians used a written language made up of pictures called:
a) Hieroglyphs
b) Hierograms

3. When ancient Egyptians died, their bodies were specially prepared for burial. They were:
a) Mummicated
b) Mummified

4. The ancient Egyptians worshiped gods and goddesses:
a) True
b) False

5. The famous ancient Egyptian Pyramids of Giza were built as:
a) Palaces
b) Tombs

6. The ancient Egyptian civilization lasted for:
a) Three thousand years
b) Three hundred years

Into the Tomb

"We can't go back to the apartment now. It'd be too risky," Zak frowned. "In fact, just going down to street level from the rooftops is going to be risky."

David glanced around. "How about we borrow some clothes from the clotheslines up here? Maybe we could leave some money so it wouldn't exactly be stealing."

"That's not a bad idea," Zak agreed. They both chose long robes and lengths of fabric they could wrap around their heads and faces to hide their features and make them look like locals. Soon they were ready to mingle with the people down below.

As they transformed themselves, Layla watched them hopefully, and inwardly Zak began to worry that he had promised her more than they would be able to deliver.

David saw the doubt cross his big brother's face, and offered another good suggestion. "Let's take a look at the facts we know," he reasoned. "Then we can make a plan. That's what spies and detectives do."

Zak nodded. "OK, you start."

David began by explaining what evidence he'd seen in the office that made him suspect Dr. Simmons was a criminal, perhaps stealing from the tomb he was supposed to be excavating.

"No wonder he hasn't publicized the tomb discovery very much. He's been taking away its treasures first," Zak concluded.

"If you were going to investigate what was going on..." David began.

"I would go to the Scorpion Tomb," Zak finished the sentence. He turned to Layla. "You must keep quiet about meeting us, OK? It's safer for you that way, but we will need to get a message to you when we find your brother," he continued.

"Every morning I take Rami to the park, by the fountain," Layla replied. "Find us there."

"OK, we will. Now go down the stairs, and we'll wait a few minutes before we do the same," Zak replied.

"Thank you for helping," Layla said shyly.

"Thank you for rescuing us," Zak smiled. "And take care of Rami—he's a great dog to have around."

After Layla had disappeared, Zak turned to David with a serious look on his face.

"Look, David. We both know this could be dangerous. I'm not sure you should..." he began, but could see from his little brother's expression what the answer was going to be.

"I'm coming and that's that," David insisted. "You may know all about hieroglyphics and stuff, but you need my practical knowledge of adventure stories, big brother."

"That's the truth," Zak grinned. They were a team now, and there was really no question. They were working together.

They climbed down to ground level and set

out for the outskirts of the town toward the Scorpion Tomb site. The walk into the open landscape was a hot and airless trudges but eventually they reached the top of a slope looking out over the desert. Beneath it was a rock face and down below they could see an entrance into the rock. In front of it an area of ruined pillars had been excavated.

"That's the entrance to the Scorpion Tomb," Zak explained. "In front of it there would once have been a courtyard lined with beautifully painted pillars. Over centuries the courtyard would have choked up with sand and hidden the entrance."

"The place looks empty," David murmured.

"Not quite. Get down out of sight!" Zak urged. A vehicle had appeared in the distance, and it was heading toward the tomb. It parked below the rock face and a tall blond man stepped out, along with some armed companions.

"Surprise, surprise. Dr. Simmons," David hissed. They watched as he directed his men to unload some boxes and carry them inside the tomb entrance. After half an hour or so

the group reappeared and drove off.

"OK, the coast's clear," David confirmed.

They made their way down to the tomb entrance and stepped inside a tunnel lined with blocks of stone. It been shored up with wooden scaffolding in places where the rock behind it had crumbled.

"Someone has put a lot of work into this excavation over quite some time. So much for 'recent discovery.' More like a discovery kept secret," Zak commented. As the meager light from the entrance faded, he picked up an electric lamp that someone had placed on the floor. When switched on, its glow revealed hieroglyphics spread over the wall surface. Zak studied a few of them.

"These hieroglyphics suggest that this was the tomb of a government official," he murmured. "They invoke the scorpion goddess several times, to help the dead person to be reborn in the afterlife, and to punish any tomb robbers."

David smiled. Zak might be impractical when it came to making tents and signaling with mirrors but as an expert on the history of ancient

Egypt, he was amazing.

"I knew it was a good idea to come to Egypt with you!" David told him, and Zak, delighted, took a little bow. "Would this official have been buried with lots of treasures?" David added, looking around curiously.

"There would certainly have been some," Zak explained. "He would be buried with all he needed for the afterlife, and if he was an important official, I imagine that he'd want a few treasures."

They ventured farther in until they reached an empty chamber that looked like the far end of the dig. They stood in the gloom. "Where are the boxes?" David wondered, feeling confused.

"Aha," Zak announced mysteriously. "The original builders would have done all they could to foil tomb robbers. They started rumors about all kinds of curses, of course, to scare raiders off."

"The curse of the mummy's tomb!" David said in a deep, spooky voice.

"Exactly. But they also built in some clever little secrets," Zak explained.

He shone the light onto a wall and focused on a block of stone.

"There it is," he said triumphantly.

The lamp illuminated a line of scorpions carved into the stone at different angles. In the center of the row there was a gap, and though part of the stone had crumbled away from that area, it was clear that there was one scorpion missing from the line at this point. Zak studied it for a moment, then moved his lamp around to illuminate other blocks that lined the wall. He studied them one by one. Each was carved with a single scorpion.

"That'll be the one...." Zak muttered.

He placed his hand on the center of one of the single scorpion carvings and pushed gently.The wall moved smoothly backwards, revealing a narrow tunnel that went sideways into the wall stone and then turned into another chamber.

"Wow!" David gasped.

"Clever people, those tomb builders," Zak grinned. They wriggled through the tunnel into the second chamber, where the lamp lit up piles of cardboard boxes.

Zak was about to speak when David clamped a hand over his mouth.

There was a noise.

They flattened themselves against the boxes and Zak hurriedly clicked off the lamp.

There it was again...a scraping sound.

Something was moving in the darkness.

Which scorpion is missing from the row of carvings in the center? Which block should Zak push to open the secret tunnel?

Do you think you'd be good at disguising yourself to avoid being recognized, like David and Zak did in Egypt? Can you choose the correct disguise tips from these options?

XTREME ADVENTURE QUIZ 7

1. To disguise yourself, would it be better to:
a) Cover your head with a hat?
b) Cover your hands with gloves?

2. When you are in disguise, and someone looks at you, should you:
a) Look straight back at them?
b) Avoid looking them in the eye?

3. If you have a choice of two disguise outfits would you choose:
a) The gray outfit?
b) The red outfit?

4. When you are putting on your disguise would it be better to:
a) Wear a set of fake teeth?
b) Change your hairstyle?

5. To change how you look would it be better to:
a) Wear a new pair of glasses?
b) Wear a new pair of shoes?

6. Which do you think is easier when using face make-up?
a) Pretending to look older?
b) Pretending to look younger?

The Scorpion Secret

"Who is it?" someone whispered in Arabic. The voice was quivering, and sounded very scared. "I am Hassan! I am armed!"

Zak clicked the lamp back on.

"Hassan? Is that you?" he asked, amazed. Sure enough, the boy from the shop appeared from behind the boxes, obviously unarmed.

"Yes!" he cried delightedly, and hugged Zak like a long-lost relative. Zak introduced him to David.

"David, this is Layla's brother. He sold me your statue."

"Layla? You know my little sister? Is she OK?" Hassan asked anxiously.

"Yes, she's fine," Zak replied. "But we need to

talk, Hassan. Tell us what's going on. Are you in big trouble?"

Hassan looked around wildly.

"Don't worry. Dr. Simmons is gone. We saw him leave with his men," Zak explained.

Hassan looked relieved, but then sat down glumly on a box. David thought he looked tired and troubled.

"Dr. Simmons is a criminal," Hassan said angrily. "At the museum they think he is a first-class excavator when really he steals the best treasures he finds and sells them to crooked collectors. Mr. Rashi, the statue shop owner, helps him sell them."

"Zak, look at this," David said. He picked something out from an open box and held it up to the light of the lamp. It shone with the unmistakable glow of gold.

Zak gasped. "It's an ancient Egyptian arm bangle. It's very fine," he murmured, examining its exquisite detail. "The only problem is, it doesn't belong in this tomb. I'm certain it's from a different period in Egyptian history."

Hassan explained. "In these boxes there is a hoard of goods from all over Egypt, not just

from this dig. The Scorpion Tomb was not rich in finds at all," he said.

Zak translated Hassan's words for David.

"Is he trustworthy?" David asked. "I get the feeling he is, but I still don't understand what he's doing here."

Zak turned back to Hassan. "Are you in Simmons's gang?" he asked bluntly.

"No, no. I only pretend I am. I must, to keep Layla safe!" Hassan cried.

"Have you been threatened?" Zak asked. Hassan's shoulders dropped and he shook his head, as if he couldn't believe how he had gotten into such a mess.

"I found out everything after I sold you the statue of the scorpion goddess. It was the real one; it was one of the few pieces that came from this tomb. It was copied by mistake when it was left in Mr. Rashi's stoneyard, and it was sent to the shop in error," he explained.

Zak translated for a fascinated David before Hassan continued his account. "When he found that I'd sold the statue, Mr. Rashi shouted at me a lot. He wanted to know who had bought it from me," Hassan said, hanging his head. "He threatened me and my family so I had to tell him. Then he vowed he would get it back from your apartment. I saw you at the café and I tried to warn you not to go back while he was there with his men. I could not speak to you because it was too dangerous for me. I am sorry."

Zak patted him on the shoulder. "So it was you who wrote the note on the bill. It was brave of you to try to warn us," he said. "And am I right in thinking you tried again later?"

Hassan nodded. "That afternoon Mr. Rashi made me go to his stonemason's yard. He said I was going to have to do some hard work to pay for my mistake with the statue. I was there when they brought you in, tied up, and I tried to warn you again."

"You whispered in English," Zak nodded.

"Yes, and I wanted to help you more, but then Dr. Simmons arrived. He was very angry about what had happened. He said that Mr. Rashi's men should never have kidnapped you, but now they must dump you in the desert to scare you and stop you from asking questions. Dr. Simmons said I could be useful to him, and I was to say nothing, or my family would be hurt,"

Hassan continued. "Now I must stay here in the tomb every night to guard the boxes. I have a lamp, and food, but it is very frightening and cold. I cannot use the lamp all night because I must save the oil, and..."

"Sshhh. I can hear something, maybe a truck engine," David warned.

Hassan looked terrified. "They have returned!" he cried. "You must go! Quickly!"

Zak put his arm on Hassan's shoulder. "Hassan, you must be very brave and stay in the gang. Otherwise, you and your family would be under great threat. Say nothing for now. We will get help."

David stepped back in the direction they had come. "No! Not that way! They will see you! This tomb has many tunnels. Here. This is a map Dr. Simmons made. Take it. Go! Through there!" Hassan gestured toward another narrow tunnel partly hidden behind the boxes.

Zak and David wriggled through into the second tunnel. They had to crouch as they moved, then switch off the lamp and stand still in the dark when they heard voices in the chamber behind them. It seemed like ages before the sound died and the lamp could go back on.

"There is another way out of the tomb according to this map," David whispered.

Zak studied the piece of paper. "All the extra tunnels marked here suggest to me that this tomb was robbed centuries ago," he murmured. "Thieves used to tunnel their way in. They would have stolen all they could find, which would explain why Dr. Simmons didn't discover much during his excavation. Your statue was probably the best piece he uncovered from the rubble."

"Not much reward for a lot of effort," David remarked.

"Exactly. I can see that the tomb makes a good storage place for other stolen goods, but I wonder why Dr. Simmons has put so much effort into clearing the rubble from these other tunnels...." Zak pondered.

They reached another widened chamber. Any treasures that might have been there were long gone, except for one or two heavy carved statues, cut from the wall itself. They looked eerie in the light, a reminder that this was once a sacred place.

Zak flashed the beam around, illuminating more tunnels leading off the chamber. "There's something strange that I don't understand...." he muttered, thinking intently.

"What is it?" David asked.

"Tombs of this date usually have a large inner burial chamber, larger than this one, yet there is no such thing marked on the map," Zak explained. He began to walk back the way they had come.

"What are you doing?" a surprised David demanded, but Zak didn't answer. He was concentrating. He had reached a section of tunnel where the ceiling was slightly higher than the rest, and shored up with extra scaffolding that hid the roof itself. He glanced up, then down to the ground.

"What are we looking for?" David whispered impatiently.

Zak held his lamp upward.

"I suspect there used to be a hole up there. It's been hidden by the scaffolding, so Dr. Simmons missed the signs. I think it was a burial shaft, where they lowered things down to...there."

He swung the light down the wall and then

across the uneven worn blocks on the floor, and finally settled the beam on a single flagstone. He smiled, set the lamp on the ground, and ran his hand across the stone's surface. Then he curled his fingers around its rough edge and pulled.

Nothing happened.

"David, you pull on the other side," he said. They combined their strength, and this time it lifted.

The light showed a gaping black hole beneath. There was some kind of staircase, badly crumbled and too dangerous to step on. Below it lay a shadowy bulk.

David gasped.

"You are looking at an ancient Egyptian coffin," Zak breathed.

They both stood in awed silence as Zak played light over bowls, jars, and statues that lay around the burial, containing the most precious items that the dead might need in the afterlife. Zak shook his head in amazement. "This chamber has not been robbed since it was sealed thousands of years ago," he murmured. "Dr. Simmons hasn't found it, but he suspects it's here."

"That's why he's been excavating all the tunnels!" David cried. "He missed it, but you found it, Zak! You're brilliant!" David congratulated him.

"I read more books than he does, I guess," Zak replied.

"You read more books that anyone," David grinned.

"This could be the most exciting find in ancient Egyptian archaeology in years," Zak murmured.

"But..." David began.

"We must seal it up again. I know," Zak finished the sentence for him. "We must get out of here in one piece, and report it. And we must make sure that Dr. Simmons doesn't get his hands on it,"

They both took one last look at the unexplored treasure chamber. Then Zak grasped the edge of the stone block. "Come on, then. Let's do it," he urged.

They pulled the stone back in place and brushed dust across it, to make it look the same as all the others. Then they continued along the tunnel, still feeling elated by what they had seen.

They reached the wide chamber once again and held the light up to the different tunnels they had to choose from as their next route.

"Which one should we take?" David muttered, studying the map.

Suddenly they heard a muffled sound from behind them.

"Someone's coming! Quick! Choose now!" Zak urged.

Imagine that you are in the same situation as David and Zak, inside an ancient Egyptian tomb with your enemy not far behind. What equipment would be most useful? Choose from these options:

XTREME ADVENTURE QUIZ 8

1. Choose between:
a) An electric flashlight
b) A solar-powered flashlight

2. Choose between:
a) A hieroglyphic translation book
b) A map of tunnels

3. Choose between:
a) Clothing to keep you warm
b) Clothing to keep you cool

4. Choose between:

a) A walking stick

b) A skateboard

5. Choose between:

a) A bottle of water

b) A roll of toilet paper

6. Choose between:

a) A pack of chewing gum

b) A baseball cap

Out in the Open

"This way," David mouthed silently, pointing to one of the tunnels. They dived into it. The voices faded behind them.

"I hope you chose the right tunnel, David," Zak thought to himself silently, but he somehow knew his little brother would have gotten it right. That was the moment when he realized he trusted David absolutely now. His younger brother's quick thinking and practicality had saved them over and over again.

David was thinking about Zak, too. "I can't believe we found secret treasure! I have the coolest brother on the planet!"

Zak switched off his lamp, yet there was still some light, natural light seeping in from around a last corner. They'd made it to an exit, a tiny opening in the rock face just big enough for them to wriggle through on their stomachs. The fresh air was a great relief after the dust-filled atmosphere in the tomb, but the sunlight was blinding. They found themselves on a high ledge above the tomb entrance. They were in full view. If Dr. Simmons came out now he would spot them immediately. They'd make an easy target against the pale stone, and there would be no escape. Just a couple of bullets would finish it.

This time they couldn't help each other. Each had to rely on his own balance and self-control. They inched their way toward ground level, finding what footholds they could. Once or twice they sent shards of loose stone rolling down, but luckily there was no one outside to hear or see.

"Ok, David?" Zak muttered as he pressed his back against the hard, sharp rock face.

"OK," David confirmed. "I've seen Indiana Jones do this sort of thing, and he always makes it," he thought to himself as he moved his foot slowly, gingerly, to another spot. "If we can just

get out of here...I'm sure there's going to be a happy ending for us too...."

His concentration wavered for a second. Suddenly his foot slipped. A rock crumbled away, as soft as cheese, and he felt himself wobbling. He clawed the wall with his fingers. His foot found another rock, and he balanced himself again. He looked over at Zak, who had turned very pale, and he smiled sheepishly.

"Just testing," he joked, but he concentrated extra-hard after that.

At last they reached the bottom and scrambled out of sight behind rocks. They had made it just in time. People were emerging from the tomb. Hassan, Dr. Simmons, and a couple of men got into the truck, looking calm and unconcerned.

"I think Hassan has pulled it off so far," David whispered. "I doesn't look as if Simmons has any idea we are nearby."

"We can't leave Hassan in jeopardy for long, though. We have to get help," Zak murmured.

"Help we can trust," David added.

They walked back toward town, keeping an eye out for the truck. Danger wasn't over for them, they knew, but they both felt buoyed up by their discovery and knew that they had enough strength, and more, between them to see this adventure through.

Nobody glanced twice at the two dusty-robed figures reentering town and hunkering down in a doorway to sleep, nor did they take much notice of the grimy pair wandering in the park the next morning.

Only Rami recognized them. He bounded up as soon as he and Layla arrived.

"Zak! David! What happened? Did you find my brother?" she asked anxiously.

"Yes we did. But we need your help one more time...." Zak replied.

*

Gama was busy feeding his camels when his children ran over, shouting, "The crazy boys are back!" Two camels were lumbering over the horizon, ridden awkwardly by none other than Zak and David in some filthy robes.

"Am I glad to see you," Zak grinned when they reached a very surprised-looking Gama. "Let's face it. I'm not good on camels. A young friend of ours brought us these two. All they've done is spit and kick. Still, we had to find you, Gama. Being friends with us is a busy job. We need more help."

That night they outlined their plans to Gama, who agreed to take them to another town, in the opposite direction from the Scorpion Tomb, a place where they could find a cell phone or maybe a computer Internet connection, and get assistance.

"I hope Hassan can stay out of trouble until we're able to rescue him," David fretted.

"He'll be OK," Zak reassured him. "I think he's proved he's pretty strong-spirited."

It was night now, and the desert sky was ablaze with stars. Zak pointed up to the North Star. "I know the name of that star, thanks to you," he remarked.

"Yes, but I know how to find priceless treasures, thanks to you," David laughed.

"I thought you were a little pain when we first came out on this vacation," Zak grinned.

"And I thought you were a total bore," David countered.

"What do you think now?" Zak asked.

"That we're brothers," David replied simply.

*

When they reached their new destination, they managed to contact their uncle in Cairo. David wisely let Zak do the talking:

"Yes, that's right. Your apartment's been trashed....Yes, we've been accused of stealing a statue....No, no. We're OK, though I got stung by a scorpion, and David nearly fell off a cliff, but...yes. Yes. Calm down, Uncle. It's going to be OK. We just need to you to phone some of your friends...."

Which tunnel should David and Zak take to get out of the tomb? Study the map to find the right one.

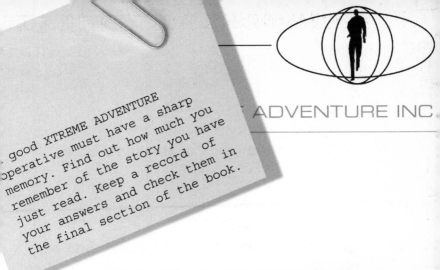

good XTREME ADVENTURE operative must have a sharp memory. Find out how much you remember of the story you have just read. Keep a record of your answers and check them in the final section of the book.

XTREME ADVENTURE QUIZ 9

1. What was the name of Hassan's dog?

2. What did Gama put on Zak's scorpion sting?

3. How did David find the direction north when he and Zak were in the desert?

4. What was the name of Hassan's little sister?

5. Was the desert cooler in the daytime or at night?

6. What did Zak use to make DIY sunglasses?

David and Zak have almost come to the end of their adventure, and you have almost finished your training. Read the following Mission Report to find out what happened next....

XTREME ADVENTURE INC.

SCORPION SECRET
MISSION REPORT

TOP SECRET

AUTHORIZED AGENTS ONLY

MISSION REPORT:

David and Zak's uncle was an old friend
of ours. In fact, he was once one of our
top agents, code-named "Indiana," and
although he is now retired, he still
does research work for us. Like all our
agents, he keeps his status quiet from
his family and friends, but now he told
his nephews the truth, and called in
XTREME ADVENTURE INC. Because of
the danger to Hassan, still undercover
in Dr. Simmons's gang, and because
of the extreme importance of the hidden
treasures of the Scorpion Tomb,
immediate action was necessary.

Situation judged **URGENT.**

Action taken:

Dr. Simmons continued with his trade in stolen
treasures, unaware that Zak and David had
discovered the truth. He assumed they
had fled the area in fear. This enabled us to
set up our operation. Our agents entered the
Scorpion Tomb and surprised Dr. Simmons
when he arrived, arresting him and gathering
plenty of evidence of his crime. At the same
time, his accomplices were arrested in the
stoneyard and statue shop. Hassan was
not arrested as a gang member. He quietly
returned home, unsuspected by those around
him of involvement. This was judged the safest
option for him.

Result: The criminal network set up by Dr.
Simmons was smashed.

Follow-up work: The private business records
of Mr. Rashi were used to trap crooked
collectors who had bought stolen goods. Stolen
artefacts were found and returned. Agent
Indiana ensured that this went smoothly.

SPECIAL EXTRA REPORT

SCORPION TOMB

The secret burial chamber found in the Scorpion Tomb was excavated by experts and found to be of great importance to the understanding of ancient Egyptian history. XTREME ADVENTURE INC. provided guards for the site during excavation.

AGENT REPORT: ZAK TURNER

Zak Turner was recommended for specialist training with XTREME ADVENTURE INC. Though lacking practical survival skills, he showed bravery and exceptional team qualities. He has good language skills and outstanding historical knowledge.

Mistakes made: Carelessness led to a scorpion sting, and to Dr. Simmons almost catching them at the museum.

Recommendation: During training, concentrate on survival skills.

Update: Following training, Zak Turner has become a top specialist expert at XTREME ADVENTURE INC. headquarters. He provides excellent back-up information for agents.

Location: XTREME ADVENTURE INC. headquarters. Occasionally works as a team in the field with agent "Scorpion."

Code-name: Bookman

Alias: University professor or tourist.

AGENT REPORT: DAVID TURNER

David Turner was recommended as ideal material for XTREME ADVENTURE INC. training. He showed quick-thinking and practicality. He was calm in a crisis and worked well in a team.

Mistakes made: At first David was intolerant of Zak, but he quickly overcame this.

Recommendation: During training, concentrate on teamwork skills.

Update: Following training David Turner has become a top operative.

Locations: Worldwide capabilities.

Code name: Scorpion

Alias: Archaeologist or tourist.

AGENT REPORT: HASSAN

Hassan was recommended for XTREME ADVENTURE training because of his bravery and outstanding undercover work. He has good language skills, local knowledge, and dog-handling ability.

Mistakes made: Went undercover with no back-up.

Recommendation: During training, concentrate on undercover skills.

Update: Following training, Hassan is an excellent operative in the field.

Location: Egypt

Code name: Stonecutter

Alias: Schoolboy

Note: Hassan's young sister, Layla, shows great promise for future training.

Note: Rami, Hassan's dog, is now an outstanding animal operative for XTREME ADVENTURE INC. He has special skills in tracking and guarding.

YOUR AGENT REPORT

Did you pass the tests as well as David and Zak? Score your answers to the puzzles and quizzes. Then take the ultimate **ELITE SQUAD** desert test on page 126.

Operative Field Test 1 (page 18)

Score 1 for each correct answer.
1. Mediterranean **2.** Alexandria **3.** Cairo
4. Pyramids at Giza **5.** Red Sea

Quiz 1 Score 1 for each correct answer.
1. a) A river **2.** b) North Africa **3.** c) A sea
4. c) Cairo **5.** b) A very dry area **6.** b) A man-made river channel.

Operative Field Test 2 (page 28)
Score 2 if you worked out this route.

Quiz 2 Score 1 for each correct answer.
1. a) Stay in a crowded street. It will be easier to escape, and less likely that your pursuer will attack you. **2.** b) Make changes of direction to confuse and lose your pursuer. **3.** b) Try to see your pursuer in window reflections. Don't look around. He won't realize you know he's there, and won't be expecting you to escape.

4. b) A restaurant will have a back door, usually in the kitchen. You can escape through it. **5.** b) Take the taxi, because you can order it to go anywhere you want, and it won't stop. A bus stops regularly, takes on other passengers, and has a known route.

6. b) Drive to a shopping center. You can park in a big parking lot and lose yourself in the crowd. Don't lead your pursuer to your home. That would be dangerous and a harder place to escape from.

Operative Field Test 3 (page 38)

Score 3 for the correct answer: Building A. Starting at the apartment, they must pass, in order, a bazaar, fountain, school, and mosque, and on the route they must go through three sets of traffic lights.

Quiz 3 Score 1 for each correct answer.
1. a) True **2.** b) False **3.** b) False
4. b) Poisonous snake **5.** a) Sandflies
6. b) Sandstorm

Operative Field Test 4 (page 52)

Score 3 for the correct answer:
Zak's symptoms match the sting of a scorpion.

Quiz 4 Score 1 for each correct answer.

1. a) Wrap something around your head. You must protect it from the sun. **2.** b) Plants grow where there is water in the ground. **3.** b) If they lie still, the poison will take longer to have an effect. If you suck it out, you could get poisoned yourself. **4.** a) Dehydration. **5.** a) In shady places. **6.** b) Long sleeves and long pants, to avoid sunburn.

Operative Field Test 5 (page 64)

Score 3 for the correct answer:
The real statue is the one lying down in the bottom right of the picture. It has a broken hand. The others are all perfect.

Quiz 5 Score 1 for each correct answer.

1. a) True **2.** a) True **3.** b) False. They use camels. **4.** b) False. They wear long robes.
5. b) False. They are likely to speak Arabic.
6. a) True. Tea is given as a ceremonial welcome to guests.

Operative Field Test 6 (page 74)

Score 3 for the correct answer:
The stolen statue is on Dr. Simmons's laptop screen. He must have photographed it and scanned the picture in. Yet the museum exhibition says that no movable statues were found in the tomb. He must have hidden it.

Quiz 6 Score 1 for each correct answer.
1. b) Pharaoh **2.** a) Hieroglyphs **3.** b) Mummified **4.** a) True **5.** b) Tombs **6.** a) 3000 years.

Operative Field Test 7 (page 86)

Score 2 for the correct answer: The block on the top left is the one to push. It shows the scorpion pointing down and to the right–the only one that is missing from the line of scorpions.

Quiz 7 Score 1 for each correct answer.
1. a) A hat will hide your face, and your identity, better. **2.** b) Avoid looking at them, so as not to draw attention to yourself. **3.** a) A gray outfit will be less obvious than a red one. **4.** b) Changing your hairstyle will change your appearance more. **5.** a) A new pair of glasses will change your face.

6. a) It's easier to look older, using make-up to add wrinkle lines and shadows. These can't easily be hidden by make-up if they are naturally there. If you are still a child or teenager, make-up makes you immediately look older.

Operative Field Test 8 (page 100)

Score 1 for each clue you spotted: The correct flagstone is the one to the front of the floor, between the scorpion's pincers.

The two clues are: **1.** On the wall beneath the statue, the same scorpion shape is shown holding a tiny square flagstone. **2.** The same scorpion and flagstone is shown on the wall above the doorway.

Quiz 8 Score 1 for each correct answer.

1. a) An electric flashlight. A solar-powered one won't work underground. **2.** b) A map of tunnels will help you get out. **3.** a) Underground tunnels are chilly. You need warm clothing. **4.** a) A walking stick will be useful for walking over uneven ground. A skateboard won't work on an uneven, rubble-strewn surface. **5.** a) Water is vital for your survival, but you can do without toilet paper. Improvise with something else if you have to. **6.** b) A cap will help keep your head warm. Chewing gum would be useless.

Operative Field Test 9 (page 110)

Score 2 for the correct answer:
Tunnel **A** is the one that will lead them out.
It starts by turning left, like the correct one
shown on the map. The others turn right.

Quiz 9 Score 1 for each correct answer.
1. Rami **2.** Yellowy paste made from crushed
plants **3.** By finding the North Star **4.** Layla
5. At night **6.** A roll of film.

Total up your score from a possible 80

Score of 1–30
You need to brush up on your skills. Better luck
next time.

Score of 31–50
You're almost ready to become an agent. Try
again with another XTREME ADVENTURE.

Score of 51–80
Well done!
You can join XTREME ADVENTURE INC!

Welcome to:
XTREME ADVENTURE INC

Now you are ready to take:

THE ELITE SQUAD DESERT TEST

Somewhere in the pictures of this book we have hidden ten little desert lizards. Find them all to join our ELITE SQUAD used for top missions.

Good luck, and see you on the next adventure!

On a trip with his parents to the Amazon, Simon suddenly finds himself alone in the depths of the rainforest. How will he communicate with the local people? What dangers lie in wait for him? And will he be able to rescue his parents from the evil gang that holds them captive? Join the action and check out your own survival skills in the next exciting XTREME ADVENTURE INC. title:

Attack of the Jaguar